MIRACLE™
ON 34ᵀᴴ STREET

MIRACLE™
ON 34TH STREET

A novelization by A.L. Singer
Based on the 1947 motion picture screenplay
by George Seaton and story by Valentine Davies
Screenplay by George Seaton and John Hughes

SCHOLASTIC INC.
New York Toronto London Auckland Sydney

TWENTIETH CENTURY FOX PRESENTS A JOHN HUGHES PRODUCTION A LES MAYFIELD FILM "MIRACLE ON 34TH STREET" RICHARD ATTENBOROUGH ELIZABETH PERKINS DYLAN McDERMOTT J.T. WALSH JAMES REMAR WITH MARA WILSON AND ROBERT PROSKY MUSIC BY BRUCE BROUGHTON COSTUME DESIGNER KATHY O'REAR EDITOR RAJA GOSNELL PRODUCTION DESIGNER DOUG KRANER DIRECTOR OF PHOTOGRAPHY JULIO MACAT EXECUTIVE PRODUCERS WILLIAM RYAN AND WILLIAM S. BEASLEY BASED UPON THE STORY BY GEORGE SEATON AND THE PLAY BY VALENTINE DAVIES SCREENPLAY BY GEORGE SEATON AND JOHN HUGHES PRODUCED BY JOHN HUGHES DIRECTED BY LES MAYFIELD
©1994 TWENTIETH CENTURY FOX

ISBN 0-590-22505-7

12 11 10 9 8 7 6 5 4 3 2 1   4 5 6 7 8 9/9

Printed in the U.S.A.   40

First Scholastic printing, December 1994

MIRACLE™
ON 34ᵀᴴ STREET

1.

"Look at him, Grandpa!" Ryan Harper said.

Judge Henry Harper frowned at his grandson. "Shhh!"

There. Waiting for the light at 77th Street and Central Park West. Reading a newspaper and holding a cane. It had to be . . . *him*!

He was old.

He had the beard — white . . . and *real*.

Red cheeks, too.

And he was here in New York City, going to the Cole's Thanksgiving Day Parade.

Who else could it be?

Ryan was practically bursting. "Ask him!" he pleaded.

Judge Harper scowled. "Ryan, that's enough!"

Looking up from his newspaper, the white-bearded man turned and smiled. Across the street, where the parade was about to start, a

1

brass band played Christmas carols.

"See!" Ryan said. "Look at him, Grandpa!"

Judge Harper laughed politely. He hoped the geezer wouldn't mind. This *was* New York City, and you never knew how people would react. . . . "I'm sorry. My grandson thinks you're Santa Claus."

The old man chuckled. He tucked his paper under his arm and patted the little boy on the head.

"I *am*."

Judge Harper's smile faded. That wasn't the response he expected.

The light turned to green. "Merry Christmas," the old man said as he crossed the street.

Ryan stared, rooted to the spot. "Wow!" he said. "I could have got his autograph."

2.

THANKSGIVING DAY, 10:22 A.M.

"I don't know why I'm doing this." A cluster of balloons bopped Dorey Walker in the face.

She pushed them aside and walked through the crowd.

COLE'S, the balloons said. The largest department store in New York. Her employer.

For now.

"I don't know *why* I'm breaking my neck on this stupid parade," Dorey went on. "Cole's is going to be taken over by Shopper's Express anyway. We'll all be out of work."

Her assistant's voice piped up, "They said in the paper that the takeover's not going to happen."

Myrna Foy wasn't much shorter than Dorey. But somehow she needed to take two steps for each one her boss took.

"Victor Lamberg owns seventy-five hundred

3

Shopper's Express stores across the country," Dorey replied. "If he wants something bad enough, he gets it. We're dead."

"What if we have a really big Christmas?" Myrna asked. "Won't that make it difficult for Lamberg to buy us?"

"A big Christmas in *these* times? Nobody has any money. Whatever they *do* have will end up in Lamberg's pocket. How do we compete?"

Myrna shrugged. "Well, we're the store that brings Santa Claus to town."

"Lamberg's worth a billion dollars. I guarantee he's not worried about Santa Claus."

Bleeep! Bleeep!

Dorey looked at her beeper. "It's my boss," she said. "Emergency."

The TV-control booth was only a few yards away, but Dorey practically had to fight her way through the crowd. She spotted her boss, Donald Shellhammer, huddled over a TV monitor. He did not look too happy.

"What's the problem?" Dorey asked.

"Your Santa Claus is wearing an old topcoat and a fedora."

"*What?*" Dorey leaned closer to the monitor.

There was a stranger on the Santa float. He was sitting inside the makeshift sleigh and reindeer display, cracking the whip.

* * *

4

Snnnnap!

The white-bearded man smiled. "It's all in the wrist, you see." He pulled in the whip, picked up his cane, and stepped off the float.

On the street stood Tony Falacchi, Cole's official Santa. He took a swig from a bottle and tucked it in his waistband. "I think we're about to shove off, old dude."

The old man's smile vanished. "You were drinking. You're intoxicated."

Tony burped. "And you're a nuisance. Gimme my whip."

His hand darted out, but the old man blocked it with his cane.

"You're a disgrace," the stranger said. "Do you know how many children are watching you right now?"

"Gimme the whip!" Tony growled.

The old man lifted the cane high. "Young man, when you put on that suit, you represent something that has great meaning and significance to people all over the world. Especially to children. I can overlook a badly made suit, an unconvincing beard, and a poorly padded tummy . . ." — he poked at Tony's red polyester Santa suit with his cane, tugged at Tony's fake beard, jabbed him in the gut, then grabbed away his bottle — ". . . but I *won't* tolerate public drunkenness. You should be ashamed of yourself!"

"Can we get a cop over here?" Tony shouted.

A nearby policeman dropped his doughnut wrapper in the trash and ambled over. He gingerly lowered the old man's cane, which was now pointing at Tony's face. "If you're not with the parade, sir, you have to get up on the sidewalk with everybody else."

"I need to see whoever is in charge and alert them to this man's drunken condition!" the old man demanded.

"Kiss my — " Tony snarled.

The old man drew back his cane — *thoonk* — right into the policeman's hand. "That's enough, gramps," the officer said. "Let's take a little walk."

Silently the old man handed back the whip. He held his head high as the cop walked him to the curb.

Tony climbed onto the float. The end of the whip twisted around his ankles. He wobbled a bit as he stood up. His pants slid off his waist, revealing the bottom of his white belly-pad.

He lifted his pants but they fell again. Cursing, he yanked out the pad and threw it.

With a dull thump, the yellowish, sweat-stained pillow fell to the street like a dead animal.

"Ewww!" a child screeched.

Faces turned toward the float. Parents and children stared in horror, first at the pad, then at Tony.

Without the fake belly, his pants fell again. Laughter swelled up around him.

"Shut up!" Tony grumbled, letting go of his waist.

PHWEEEEEEET! trilled a drum major's whistle.

The parade was beginning!

His pants around his feet, Tony bellowed, *"Merry Christmas to all, and to all a good night!"*

He raised the whip handle. The whip pulled on his ankles.

Out went Tony's feet.

He flipped into the air. With a *whomp*, he landed on the sleigh floor.

Ping! Ping! Ping! Ping!

At once, the bolts holding the sleigh to the float sprang off.

Dorey Walker stood at the curb, gaping. "Oh, no!" she whispered as she watched the entire sleigh slowly topple to the street.

3.

THANKSGIVING DAY, 10:31 A.M.

"**H**eeeee-yah-ha-ha-ha-ha!"

He was laughing. That drunken sot was lying on the street in his Cole's Santa suit and *laughing*.

Dorey was horrified. She hoped no news cameras were around. Cole's was having enough trouble as it was. This would be a disaster for the store's image.

Workers were lifting the sleigh back onto the float. But as far as Dorey was concerned, Tony was history. He couldn't go back up. Not in this state.

"Officer!" she called to the nearest policeman. "There was an older man on the float a few minutes ago. Did you see him?"

"Yeah, he was just here," the policeman said. "You're the Cole's lady?"

Dorey nodded.

"He wanted to talk to you." The policeman pointed across the street. "That's him. In the old coat."

"Thanks."

The old man was walking into Central Park. *A little shabby, but neat*, Dorey thought. Not a bum. He might be able to handle it. She ran across the street, scooping up Tony's Santa hat on the way.

"Sir?" she shouted.

The man turned around.

"I'm Dorey Walker, Director of Special Projects for C. F. Cole and Company." She extended her hand.

"My pleasure," the man replied. "I was looking for you. As you probably saw, your Santa Claus is drunk."

"I know. He's created a terrible problem. Millions of kids are watching, here and on television. They're expecting to see Santa Claus — and now we don't have one." Dorey looked him square in the eye. "Would you be our Santa Claus?"

"Me? Surely there are other people you could ask."

"Sir, the parade's already started. It's you, right now, or there's no Santa in the parade. If you want, you can have the job at the store, too."

"Can I have a moment to think about it?"

"Sure." Dorey looked at her watch for a moment. "Okay, time's up."

"I'll do it — but starting tomorrow, I must wear

9

my own suit. I'll bring it with me to work."

"A deal." She took his hand and led him back to the parade. "Now, there's nothing to worry about. Just be yourself. You'll be fine, Mister . . . ?"

"Kringle. Kriss Kringle."

Dorey laughed. "Uh-huh. Of course."

They wound their way through the crowd. In the center of the street, the workers had repaired the sleigh. Dorey helped the old man up.

She crossed her fingers. This guy could be a dud. Without a costume, without practice . . .

But something happened as he sat in the seat. His eyes seemed to dance with delight. His rounded back straightened out. And boy, did he know how to crack a whip.

Snnnnap!

It resounded like a shot.

"Now, Dasher! Now, Dancer! Now, Prancer and Vixen! On, Comet! On, Cupid! On, Donder and Blitzen!"

Even his *voice* was different — strong and booming. Around her, children's and parents' eyes were riveted on the old man.

Dorey was thrilled. She ran back to the TV network booth. Shellhammer was there, grinning at the monitor.

"This Santa Claus is fantastic," he said. "Did he sign a contract?"

"There wasn't time," Dorey replied. "Myrna's

going to have him sign after the parade. He'll start work in the morning. The only condition he insisted on is that he be able to wear his own suit."

Shellhammer looked at her, amazed. "He has a Santa suit?"

"Apparently. If it's horrible, we'll make him wear ours." Dorey picked up her bag and slung it over her shoulder. "Okay, I've done my job. I'm going home. See you tomorrow."

As Dorey walked home, she didn't bother glancing upward to see the families gathered at their windows, watching the parade.

If she had, she might have seen one angry, bitter face gazing out.

The face of Victor Lamberg.

Lamberg had not made his fortune by being kind. He was vicious, rotten, and unforgiving. And it all showed in the pinched lines of his craggy face.

"Mr. Lamberg?" his maid asked softly as she entered his study. "Your grandchildren have arrived . . . to watch the parade."

But Lamberg did not turn around. His eyes were focused on the Santa Claus — and on the radiant faces of the crowd.

This was not part of the plan.

He nodded slightly, and the maid quickly left.

A few blocks away, Dorey breezed into her apartment. She gave the entryway a quick glance.

Perfect, as always. Spotless walls, tasteful paintings, all colors perfectly balanced. Like a museum.

Which was just the way Dorey liked it.

"Susan?" Dorey called out.

She walked into the living room. On the TV, a 35-inch-diagonal freeze-frame of her six-year-old daughter smiled at her.

Dorey hit PLAY on the Handycam above the TV.

Susan's video image came to life. "Mom," she said, "I'm still at Mr. Bedford's. We can see the parade from his window." Susan's face loomed closer to the camera, and she whispered, "He's really into parades. I'm doing it for him. I'd rather watch it on TV. It's more real that way. So slip into something comfortable and come over. Oh, P.S. Mr. Bedford put the turkey in the oven." Her face leaned even closer. "He said you forgot to sew up the turkey. The stuffing'll all fall out. He told me not to say anything because he *looooves* you and wants to *kiiiiiss* — "

At that point a man's arm reached into the frame, and the video went dark.

Dorey turned off the VCR. She frowned. If Susan thought she was going to be a matchmaker, she had another think coming.

In a small apartment down the hall, Bryan Bedford sipped his coffee as he watched the parade.

Susan Walker turned away from the window and said, "You know how much it costs to make

12

this parade? One point six million — and it's probably a big mistake, because some guy's going to buy Cole's and turn it into a junk store."

"Where'd you hear that?" Bryan asked.

"My mom."

Bryan shook his head. "It's not going to happen. Two big banks came in and rescued Cole's."

"But Cole's has to pay them back, plus interest," Susan said. "If they don't sell a lot of stuff at Christmas, you can forget about it, pal."

"Well, you know what? I think you should ask Santa Claus to give Cole's an interest-free loan for Christmas."

"Ha. That's a good one." Susan gave Bryan a gentle pat on the knee. "Mr. Bedford? May I call you Bryan?"

"I told you you could."

"Bryan. You know what? I know the secret — about Santa Claus. He's not real. I've known for a long time."

"Says who?" Bryan asked.

Susan turned to the window again. "My mom."

Bryan sighed. He remembered being six — almost thirty years ago. Back then, he'd believed in Santa Claus. He could barely sleep on Christmas Eves. But he always did, and Santa always came. Like magic.

Oh, well. That was a long time ago. Kids were different now.

Maybe.

Dingdong!

Bryan put down his coffee cup and answered the front door.

"Hi," Dorey greeted him. "You have something of mine?"

"About four-foot-two, dark hair? Talks like she's sixty-four years old?"

Dorey smiled and walked into Bryan's living room. "What do you think of the parade?" she asked Susan.

"It's a good one," Susan replied.

"Santa Claus come by yet?"

"Nope. Is it Tony Falacchi?"

"Tony had to leave."

Susan raised her eyebrows. "Bombed?"

"Yeah."

"It's the pressure."

"I got a new guy at the last minute," Dorey went on. "He looks like the real thing."

"Maybe he is," Bryan suggested.

Dorey grinned. "Are you still coming for dinner?"

"You bet," Bryan replied.

"Susan, run home and put that video camera stuff away, okay?" Dorey asked. "I want to talk to Mr. Bedford a minute."

"Let her finish watching the parade. Santa hasn't even come by yet," Bryan said. Then he called to Susan, "I'll put the stuff away. You keep watching."

14

Susan shrugged. "Okay."

Dorey shot Bryan a sharp look. "As soon as Santa goes by, Susan, you come home."

"Sure," Susan replied. "That's the end of the parade, anyway. There's nothing else to see except guys cleaning up after the horses. And that doesn't thrill me at all."

Dorey spun angrily away from Bryan. He followed her out the front door and down the hall to her apartment.

She was still fuming when they walked in.

"I suspect I said or did something you don't agree with," Bryan began.

"First," Dorey snapped, "what if I had called Susan from the parade and got no answer? I would have had to come home."

"We left a message on your answering machine," Bryan replied.

"Second. I'm the parent. You're the friendly guy down the hall. When I ask Susan to do something, it really doesn't help for you to offer her an alternative."

"I'm sorry. I just thought she might want to watch the parade."

"She's been watching the parade since she was two! It's the same thing every year!"

Dorey stormed into the kitchen. She yanked down the oven door and looked inside. Sure enough, he had sewn up the turkey.

"I corrected your mistake." Bryan chuckled. "I'm an attorney. I can't help it."

Now Dorey was grimacing at some brown lumps in a saucepan on the stove.

"That's the neck and the gizzard," Bryan volunteered. "You know, for giblet gravy?"

"You brought it over?"

"Uh, no. It was in the turkey. You forgot to take it out before you stuffed it. I figured, if you forgot to sew up the bird, you might have forgotten to remove the giblets. It's a common mistake."

"You *unstuffed* my turkey? You made me look like a fool by taking apart my dinner in front of my kid?"

"No, I took a plastic bag of guts out of it. You want to eat that?" Bryan took a deep breath. "Look, I'm sorry. I like Susan. A lot. I don't mean to get in your way. I have the best intentions for her. And for you, too — if you'd allow me to express them."

"Don't get the horse before the cart, Bryan." Dorey quickly looked away. "Susan had a father once. Briefly. She doesn't have one now. And there's a reason for that."

"You can think what you want about me, Dorey. And I honestly don't know what that is. After two years of seeing you, I still don't even have a hint. I'm not playing father with your daughter. Or husband with you. I'm just doing what comes naturally."

Dorey slumped onto a kitchen stool. "I apologize. I'm tired. It's been a terrible month and who knows what's going to happen — "

Bryan looked at her with concern. "You're talking about the takeover?"

"Sales were soft all spring, summer, and fall. If Christmas isn't huge, we're done."

"I don't suppose you're the type of woman who believes in miracles?" Bryan asked gently.

Dorey smiled. "No."

Looking out Bryan's window, Susan yawned. *Finally. Here comes the dumb Santa float, and then I can go have some turkey.*

The new guy looked pretty good. Real-looking beard. Only wearing an old overcoat, though. Must not have fit into Tony's getup.

The old man waved to the crowd, then looked up.

Susan felt a shiver run up her spine. He was looking at *her*. Out of the hundreds of windows on the buildings of Central Park West, he was looking at her!

And winking.

Susan sank below the windowsill. How creepy.

4.

THANKSGIVING DAY, 11:27 A.M.

Victor Lamberg sat at his desk, his eyes fixed on the TV screen. The Santa float was pulling up in front of Cole's department store now. A swarm of people clotted the sidewalk — one block away from Shopper's Express, which was deserted.

He knew that his store would lose business on this day. He wondered how much.

"What's the crowd estimate?" he barked into his phone.

On the other end, standing in front of Cole's, was Jack Duff. Duff was Lamberg's chief of operations. Some people called him slimy. Lamberg preferred the word *loyal*.

"Cops say over a million," Duff's voice replied. "Last year it was about seven hundred fifty thousand."

Lamberg frowned. "Have the marketing department come up with a giveaway, something free. I don't want a mob outside Cole's in the morning."

"I hate to say this, Mr. Lamberg," Duff said, "but Cole's has one heck of a Santa Claus this year. If I didn't know better, I'd say he was the real article."

"You told me he was the same man they used last year!" Lamberg snapped. "You said he was a drunk."

"I saw him this morning. They must have switched him at the last minute for this new guy."

The door crashed open behind Lamberg. "Grandfather!" screamed Lamberg's four-year-old granddaughter. "I saw Santa Claus! He was right outside! I waved to him!"

Lamberg put his hand over the receiver. "That's very nice, Patrice. Grandfather will be with you in a moment."

"They said on TV that he's staying at Cole's while he's in New York," Patrice gushed. "That's right by *our* store!"

She raced back out.

Lamberg's face hardened. "Keep an eye on this, Mr. Duff," he said into the phone. "I don't want my plans damaged by an elderly cherub in a red suit."

"I'm on it, sir," Duff replied.

Lamberg slammed down the phone.

Bryan cut into the turkey with a carving knife. Juice flowed down the steaming, brown-glazed side of the bird.

Susan's mouth watered. "This is kind of like TV," she said. "Except I'd need a brother and a dog. And Bryan — "

"Mr. Bedford," Dorey corrected her.

"He said I could call him Bryan," Susan protested.

"Only if it's okay with your mother," Bryan quickly added. He passed Susan a plate of turkey.

"Fine," Dorey said sharply.

"Bryan would be the dad," Susan continued. "You'd be the mom, and we'd need either a kind of fat person who's our cook or a neighbor who's always at our house."

"Uh, can we talk about something else?" Dorey asked.

Bryan held out a full plate to Dorey. "For the chef."

"The vegetables are catered," Susan remarked. "So is the dessert."

"*Thank* you, Susan," Dorey said with a sneer.

Bryan filled his own plate, then sat. "Do we give blessings in this home?"

"Not unless my grandparents are here," Susan answered.

"Would you mind if I did it?" Bryan asked. "It's kind of a tradition with me."

Dorey hesitated. "Go ahead."

Bryan and Susan lowered their heads. Reluctantly, Dorey did, too.

"We give our thanks for the warmth of this shelter, the food before us, and the closeness of the people we love," Bryan said. "We pray that these gifts we so gratefully receive might be shared many times over with those less fortunate than us."

Susan glanced up. Her mom's head was still bowed.

"Amen," Susan said — quietly, so Dorey wouldn't hear.

While they were praying, the man who called himself Kriss Kringle walked quietly home through the park.

5.

NOVEMBER 25, 8:59 A.M.
30 DAYS TO CHRISTMAS

Kids squirmed. Parents took deep breaths. The morning was clear and cloudless, and Broadway was packed, from 33rd to 34th streets. All eyes were on the enormous clock above the entrance to Cole's.

It was one minute before the official opening of the Christmas season.

On the eighth floor, Santa's Workshop was ready for action. A pathway wound through a snow-dappled village of busy mechanical elves, reindeer, and gingerbread houses.

For the next thirty days, kids from all over the world would walk down this path to see Santa Claus.

And Kriss Kringle was ready for them.

He was dressed in the finest scarlet wool flannel, sewn with gold thread and cuffed with fur. Eight sterling buttons fastened his coat, each containing the name of a reindeer. His boots were genuine leather, polished but well-worn. He wore a long black cape, fastened at the neck by a clasp with the word NOEL spelled out in sapphire chips. Every detail of Kringle's outfit was *right* — down to the gold, wreath-shaped ring on his finger.

As he sat on the throne, his "helpers" all smiled at him. They were Cole's employees, dressed as elves — and they did not miss Tony Falacchi. Not one bit.

As the clock hand inched toward 9:00, they took their places. Denice and Tricia, two of the helpers who were also best friends, leaned in to each other. "Where'd they get this guy?" whispered Denice.

Tricia shrugged. "Don't know, but I hope they can keep him."

BONNNNG!

The front doors opened. People rushed in like a herd of wildebeest.

Kriss Kringle heard the eighth-floor elevator door open. The silence was broken by squeals of anticipation.

And by his own loud, merry, "Ho-ho-ho!"

At the same time, across the street, Shopper's Express opened its doors, too. Rock-and-roll Christmas carols blared onto the sidewalk. An electronic sign, built into the glass-and-steel entrance, flashed:

OPEN TWENTY-FOUR HOURS A DAY!
FREE COFFEE!
FREE GUM GUNS!

Clack! Gulp.

Clack! Gulp.

Store workers stood outside the door, shooting gum into each other's mouths with plastic pistols.

Parents and children walked by in droves — and went straight across the street to Cole's.

A homeless man straggled over to Shopper's Express. "Cup of coffee?" he asked hopefully.

"Outta here!" snarled a worker.

The man shuffled away.

Inside a mother walked her daughter through the toy department. INTERACTIVE SANTA THIS WAY! a sign blinked. They shielded their eyes against the harsh, neon-lit displays, and walked around the stacks of boxes crowding the aisles.

Dzzzzit! Dzzzzit! All around them, electronic action figures zapped each other with guns.

Finally they reached Santa — a huge TV monitor. On it was the image of a young man with a goatee and red baseball cap. "What's up?" he asked.

"Tell Santa what you want," the mother urged her daughter.

The girl shook her head shyly.

"Maybe she'd like a Santa of her own gender,"

the image chirped. "You can punch up a She-Santa on the control panel."

"Do you want a woman Santa, sweetheart?" the mother asked.

The little girl looked lost and bewildered. She shook her head no.

Twenty stories up, Lamberg was watching. On his closed-circuit monitor, he saw the mom and daughter talking to the video. And he frowned.

Jack Duff shifted uncomfortably on Lamberg's sofa. He shot a glance at Alberta Leonard, Director of Marketing. She was sweating.

Lamberg swiveled away from the TV monitor and looked out the window. "Cole's is jammed. We're empty."

"They just had their parade," Alberta said. "Their awareness is through the roof. We'll catch up. Our polls indicate that people don't *want* a traditional Christmas. *Excitement*, *speed*, and *price* dictate where holiday money will be spent. Cole's Christmas strategy will fail."

"When?" Lamberg demanded.

"Our advertising just started," Alberta replied.

Duff chimed in, "Why couldn't we put a traditional Santa in our setting?"

"Will you let our program play out a little?"

Alberta snapped. "Cole's Santa is too old, too fat. *It won't work.*"

For the next few days, the line of children at Santa's Workshop was tremendous.

"Dorothy," Kriss Kringle said to a little girl on his knee. "That's a lovely name. One of my elves is married to a gal named Dorothy. Do you know what you want for Christmas?"

"Yep," Dorothy replied. "A Patty Pollywog Transmutable Baby Frog that swims and sings."

Kriss Kringle chuckled. "Those are a lot of fun."

"Psssssst!"

The old man looked to his left. Dorothy's mom was shaking her head no. She leaned closer to him and whispered, "Don't make me look bad. Those things are seventy bucks. My husband's on half-pay. I can't afford it."

Softly, so that Dorothy wouldn't hear, Kriss Kringle replied, "Shopper's Express has them on sale for thirty-four ninety-nine with a five-dollar rebate. Is that reasonable?"

"Yes, thanks! Since when does Cole's send customers someplace else?"

"It doesn't really matter who sells the toys, so long as the children are happy," Kringle whispered. "And I'm sure that the good people at this store believe exactly as I do."

A warm smile spread across the mother's face. "That's the spirit."

"Now, Dorothy," Kringle said to the girl, "if you're a good girl and do what your mother says, you're going to have a Patty Pollywog."

Shellhammer beamed. He hadn't seen crowds like this in years. But his favorite part was standing by the exit, watching the expressions on the children's faces. They were ecstatic.

"You the boss?" a woman called out to him.

"I'm the general manager," Shellhammer replied.

"My kid asked Santa Claus for a Barf Gun. They're ninety bucks without batteries or barf!"

"Prices do go up," Shellhammer said.

"Not at Bargain Village. Fifty-two fifty, and they throw in the batteries — according to your Santa Claus."

"Excuse me?" Shellhammer asked. He was sure he hadn't heard right.

"Your Santa's telling people where to go to shop. If you don't have it here, or it's too expensive, he's sending people to where they can get it, and at the right price."

Suddenly Shellhammer was feeling faint. "Ma'am, could you excuse me for a moment?"

His mind reeling, he darted down the hallway.

Kriss Kringle, indeed.

This man had to be fired at once!

6.

"You tell your Santa he made a Cole's shopper out of me!" the woman yelled after Shellhammer. "I'm coming here for everything but toilet paper and bananas."

Shellhammer stopped short. He turned slowly around.

"Any store that puts a parent ahead of the almighty dollar at Christmas deserves *my* business," she continued, grinning. "You tell Mr. Cole, if he's still alive, that his Santa Claus ought to get a raise!"

With a friendly wave, she walked away.

Shellhammer watched her go. Thoughts jumbled around in his head.

Then he sped off — toward Dorey Walker's office.

He pushed the door open. "Santa Claus just

28

gave me a great idea! Listen: What can we offer shoppers the discount places can't?"

Dorey looked up from her laptop, startled. "Uh . . . higher prices."

"*Service*. And why are we different?"

"Higher prices?" Dorey asked.

"We *care*," Shellhammer barged on. "We're not some big barn full of bargains where you can't get a question answered. We offer friendly, traditional service. We're a company you can trust. And do you know how we prove it?"

"Lower prices."

"No! If Cole's doesn't have what you're looking for, we'll find it for you — even if it means sending you somewhere else. How's *that* sound?"

"Sounds like a great way to go out of business," Dorey remarked.

"Mr. Kringle's been doing it all morning and we've had nothing but compliments. We're going to the chairman with it."

Dorey's jaw dropped. "We?"

"Mr. Cole *loves* you. He listens to you about things like this. If we don't turn this store around, we're all gone — from the chairman to the janitor."

"I don't know. . . ."

Shellhammer leaned forward, his eyes blazing. "Do we save this grand old store, or do we see it stripped of everything but its name?"

Dorey thought for a moment. Then she slammed her laptop shut. "Let's go."

Across from Mr. Cole's long desk, Dorey could feel her knees shaking. It hadn't taken long to pitch their idea. But Cole was taking an hour to respond.

Well, at least it *felt* like an hour.

The dark mahogany walls seemed to be closing in. The office was like a museum of antiques — and Mr. Cole was one of them.

Cole was old. He was also heavy, and from the expression on his face, you'd think he had permanent indigestion. He leaned over his desk and glared over his wire-rimmed glasses.

"I like it," he growled. "It's bold. It's fresh. It'll drive Victor Lamberg nuts."

Dorey felt like screaming with joy.

"Can you be ready with this for the morning paper?" Cole asked.

Dorey gulped. *The morning paper?* Hoo, boy. This was going to be a long night.

7.

NOVEMBER 30, 9:05 A.M.
25 DAYS TO CHRISTMAS

HOW SANTA CLAUS
CHANGED THE WAY
COLE'S DOES BUSINESS!

Lamberg scanned the newspaper ad — "service" . . . "truth" . . . "referrals to other stores" . . . "no pressure" . . .

And signed at the bottom by C. F. Cole!

Lamberg slammed his fist on his desk. "Why didn't *you* think of this?"

Jack Duff and Alberta Leonard stood across his desk, staring numbly at him.

"If this campaign is successful, Cole's is going to make a lot of money," Lamberg bellowed. "The more money they make, the harder it is for us to buy them out. I want something done about this!"

Duff and Alberta nodded so hard, Lamberg could feel the breeze.

Susan and Bryan were next in line at Santa's Workshop. Kriss Kringle was talking to a little boy, nodding deeply. The boy's mother stood nearby, dressed in a faded cloth coat that was torn but carefully mended.

"This seems like a pretty pointless exercise, Bryan," Susan said.

"Well, we were in the store, so I figured you might as well say hello to the old guy," Bryan replied.

"Why?"

"Let's just say, for the sake of argument, that there *is* a Santa Claus and you don't believe in him," Bryan said. "Is it worth the risk that you might not get anything for Christmas?"

Susan shrugged. "I didn't believe in him last year, and I got everything I asked my mother for, except for the overly violent and antisocial stuff."

"Well . . . you can get a free candy cane," Bryan tried.

"I'm trying to limit my intake of sugar."

Bryan nodded. *This girl is some tough cookie,* he thought.

Neither of them noticed the little boy hop off Kriss Kringle's lap. Nor did they see Kringle whisper to the mother, "Your son wants a bicycle.

They're very expensive, but I want him to have one."

He reached into a pocket, pulled out a crisp, hundred-dollar bill, and put it in her hand.

Tears welled up in her eyes. She leaned over and gave the kind old man a kiss. "You *are* the real Santa Claus."

As the woman left, Bryan nudged Susan forward.

She stuck out her hand for him to shake. "Hello, sir."

Kriss Kringle grinned and shook her hand. Then he gently patted his knee, and Susan climbed onto it.

"What's your name?" he asked.

"Susan Walker. What's yours?"

"Mine? I have many names. Kriss Kringle. Santa Claus. Father Christmas. St. Nicholas. In Holland I'm *Sinterklaas*. In Italy, *Befana*. I have to speak many languages because I travel a lot."

"My mom is Mrs. Walker, who runs the parade," Susan said. "I know how all this works. You're an employee of Cole's. But you're a very good Santa Claus. Your beard's realistic."

"That's because it's real. Give it a tug."

Susan pulled on the beard and nodded. Then she asked, "Your suit isn't the regular one, is it?"

"This is the *real* Santa suit," he said cheerfully.

Susan narrowed her eyes.

"Ask your dad if I'm real," Kringle suggested.

"I don't know where my dad is. That guy's my friend, Mr. Bedford. I don't have a dad anymore."

Kringle's brow creased. He nodded and cleared his throat. "Well . . . what would you like me to bring you for Christmas?"

"Nothing. My mother buys my gifts. If I don't want something too stupid or dangerous or — "

Susan suddenly stopped. Dorey was marching grimly toward them.

"Nice to see you again," Dorey said coldly to Kringle. "Susan, I think you've taken enough of the man's time. There's a very long line of customers. *They* come first."

Susan took her mom's hand and jumped off Kringle's lap.

"Nice to meet you, Susan," he said.

"Nice to meet you, too."

As they walked away, Bryan gave Kringle an embarrassed smile. "Nonbelievers."

Kringle nodded politely. Then he watched Bryan tag along after Dorey and Susan.

He sighed and signaled for the next child in line.

Dorey and Susan zigzagged through customers. "Are you mad?" Susan asked.

"No," Dorey said angrily.

"He's a nice old man. You know, his whiskers are real."

"Lots of men have real whiskers."

Bryan ran up behind them. "Dorey?" he called out. "I'm sorry. The baby-sitter wasn't feeling well, and she asked me if I'd bring Susan here. I figured we might as well say hello to Santa Claus."

"I didn't mind," Susan insisted. "It was kind of fun."

The three of them entered the outer section of Dorey's office. "Susan, would you mind sitting here with Myrna for a moment while I talk to Mr. Bedford?" Dorey asked.

Asked? It was more like *commanded*. Susan sank down on a chair opposite Myrna's desk while Bryan and Dorey went into the inner office.

Dorey closed the door behind her. She sat at her desk and crossed her arms. "If it mattered that she saw Santa Claus, I'd be more than happy to take her."

"I didn't see any harm in her saying hello to an interesting old gentleman," Bryan replied.

"There *is* harm," Dorey retorted. "*I* tell her there's no Santa Claus. *You* bring her down here and she sees thousands of gullible kids and meets a very good actor with a real beard and a beautiful suit, sitting smack-dab in the middle of a child's fantasy world. Who does she believe? The myth or the mom?"

"I'm sorry." Bryan hung his head and walked toward the door. "I'm here. I can help. All you have to do is ask."

"Will you please take Susan home with you?" Dorey asked.

With a nod, Bryan left the inner office and shut the door.

Dorey sat still for a few moments. This Santa was good, she thought. *Too* good.

She opened her desk drawer and pulled out the old man's employment file. She couldn't help but smile at the jolly photo of him.

Then she began to read:

NAME: KRISS KRINGLE
ADDRESS: MT. CARMEL SENIOR CENTER
                   124 W. 114TH STREET
                   NEW YORK, NY

Her eyes stopped when they reached the next line:

AGE: 441.

8.

NOVEMBER 30, 8:23 P.M.

Jack Duff and Alberta Leonard tiptoed into the Central Park Zoo. They followed Kriss Kringle into the reindeer section. Quietly they hid behind a bush and listened.

Kringle took some carrots out of his pocket and stuck them through the fence. A reindeer ambled over.

"The reason I haven't been by to see you is I'm working at Cole's," Kringle said to the reindeer. "All I have to do is be myself. But more important, I guess, is that I'll be doing what I most need to do — prove myself."

Duff and Alberta walked slowly into the light and approached the old man from behind.

"People don't have the faith they once had," Kringle continued. "If I can help restore some of that it will be well worth it."

"Excuse me," Duff interrupted. "My name is

Jack Duff, and this is Alberta Leonard."

Kringle turned around. "Good evening. I'm Kriss Kringle."

Duff and Alberta smiled at the joke — until the expression on Kringle's face told them it was no joke.

"We're with Shopper's Express," Duff explained. "We'd like you to be our main Santa Claus. We have over seven thousand stores worldwide, but you'd be our number-one guy."

"There's only one true Santa Claus, of course," Kringle said.

"Right. But we want you," Alberta replied. "We work for Victor Lamberg, Chairman of Shopper's Express. He's a big fan of yours. He'll pay you twice what you're making at Cole's, plus take care of you for the whole year."

"I'm very sorry," Kringle said. "I've given my word and put my signature to a contract. I can't help you." He looked at his watch. "It's getting rather late and I have a ways to go before I'm home. Merry Christmas."

"Would you like a ride?" Duff offered. "Where are you going?"

"West 114th Street," Kringle answered. "Mount Carmel Senior Center."

"We're going right by it!" Alberta shot back.

She and Duff escorted Kringle to the street, where a limousine was waiting. The three of them climbed inside.

"So tell me, Santa," Duff said, "how can one guy go to every house around the world in one night?"

"That is a vexing question, isn't it?" Kringle chuckled. "If you were able to slow time down so that a second was like a year and a minute like a century and an hour like a millenium, you'd be able to do it quite easily, wouldn't you? I must say, a hundred years ago, before the population exploded, I could deliver all my goods and have time for a late dinner, a nap, and a game of golf with the Easter Bunny. Now, of course, I haven't a moment to spare."

"I guess not," Alberta said.

She and Duff exchanged a look that said, *Weirdo.*

The limo pulled up to a crumbling brownstone on West 114th Street. Kringle thanked Duff and Alberta, then walked into the building.

"He's completely out of his mind," Albert remarked.

"Imagine Cole's hiring a guy as nutty as that." Duff smiled slyly. "It could become a *problem* for them."

Alberta nodded. "I know what you mean."

A nutcase. Mentally unstable.

If they could prove it — in public — Cole's would have a lot of explaining to do.

9.

NOVEMBER 30, 11:01 P.M.

"This holiday season, Cole's department store just may change the way New Yorkers and the world will shop," a TV reporter was saying.

Victor Lamberg could not unclench his jaw. Cole's Santa was the lead story on the 11:00 news. *The lead story!*

Now the reporter was in front of Santa's Workshop, interviewing shoppers. "Santa Claus sent me to another store because Cole's didn't carry what I wanted," said one shopper. "I was amazed."

Another said, "They're not just doing it in the toy department. I wanted a pair of boots. The guy in the shoe department sent me to a shop down the block."

Next, the Santa himself appeared on the screen. "Christmas is the time of year when we should go out of our way to help others," he said with a twinkly smile. "A corporation should do the same for its customers."

The camera cut to the reporter again. "Well, I know where *I'm* going to be doing *my* shopping this Christmas." She turned to a group of kids who'd gathered around her. "How about *you* guys?" she asked.

"*CO-O-O-OLE'S!*" the kids screamed.

Lamberg was seeing red.

The next day, Cole's was jammed. Dorey and Shellhammer looked down at Santa's Workshop from a balcony.

"You don't think he's nuts?" Dorey asked. "He absolutely believes he's Santa Claus."

"So what?" Shellhammer said. "Our sales are up seventy percent. In a week, the company has turned around."

"And we could turn the other way just as fast if this guy does something wrong. I mean, you can't rest the fate of the whole company on one very unstable old man."

"I'm not worried," Shellhammer replied.

They both looked at Kringle again.

He was using sign language to speak to a hearing-impaired girl on his knee.

In a nook of the workshop, Susan watched him with amazement. The little girl's fingers were flying gracefully in the air, and so were Kringle's.

41

Both of them laughed at whatever they were saying.

Then Kringle's eyes caught Susan's, and he winked.

Susan ducked into the shadows.

Uptown, Jack Duff and Alberta Leonard were having a conference with the director of the Mount Carmel Senior Center.

"It's awfully nice of you people at Cole's to hire Kriss," said the director, Dr. Douglas Pierce.

"We're happy to have him," Duff lied. "We only came down because we need a little background on him, and we didn't want to embarrass him."

"Yes, well, he is a bit eccentric," Dr. Pierce said.

"Yeah," Duff replied. "Do you know if he has a record of mental problems? Has he been institutionalized? Are there any situations where he might turn violent?"

"I don't know much of Kriss's history," Dr. Pierce answered. "He arrived just after Christmas last year and said he'd like to move in. And I must tell you, Mr. Duff, people are institutionalized when they pose a threat to themselves or others. Mr. Kringle wants only to be helpful and friendly. As an expert in geriatrics, I believe Kriss does not possess any dangerous tendencies."

"We don't want to deprive Mr. Kringle of something that obviously gives him great pleasure,"

Duff said. "But you have to understand Cole's position."

"Of course." Dr. Pierce nodded. "As long as he's not unreasonably provoked or ridiculed for his beliefs, he's going to be fine."

Unreasonably provoked.

Duff sneaked a glance at Alberta. That was just what they wanted to hear.

10.

Susan stood in the living room archway. She hadn't expected to see her mom on the couch at this hour. Oh, well, better sneak back into the bedroom.

"Susan? What are you doing out of bed?"

Too late. "Something's driving me crazy and I can't sleep," Susan replied.

She walked into the room and plopped onto the couch next to her mom.

"What's on your mind?" Dorey asked.

"Santa Claus," Susan said. "Mr. Kringle. He talked sign language with a kid today. It's weird how he knows so much about toys and kids. He speaks Russian and Japanese."

"He might be a very learned man."

"He looks exactly like every picture of Santa Claus I ever saw. Are you *positive* he's not the real Santa?"

44

"He fits the type, Susan. That's why I chose him." Dorey let out a deep sigh. "We've talked about Santa Claus. You understand what he is."

"What if we're wrong? That would be extremely rude. And besides, all of my friends believe in Santa Claus."

"A lot of kids your age do."

Susan frowned. "How come *I* don't?"

"Because you know the truth," Dorey replied. "And truth is the most important thing in the world. Believing in myths and fantasies makes people unhappy."

"Did you believe in Santa Claus when you were my age, and were you unhappy?"

"I did believe, and when all of the things I believed in turned out not to be true, I was very unhappy." Dorey smiled. "Look, you can believe what you want to believe. If I'm wrong, I'll admit it. Next time you see Mr. Kringle, ask for something you'd never ask me for. Then, if you don't get it for Christmas, you'll know the honest truth about Santa Claus. Okay?"

"Okay, Mom." Susan stood up. "Good night."

"Good night."

Susan walked to her bedroom, but her mind was spinning with an idea. Something that would settle the truth once and for all.

On the morning of December 12, television cameras swarmed all over the Cole's employee locker

45

room. *Good Morning America* was about to interview Kriss Kringle.

Dorey helped him put on his cape. "Just be yourself," she encouraged him. "Don't think about the camera."

"I must confess," Kringle said. "I don't understand this fuss being made over me. To most people, I'm just an old man with a beard."

"But you're still the symbol of the holiday season."

Kringle looked at her evenly. "You think I'm a fraud, don't you? And so does your daughter."

"Well, I don't think there's any harm in not believing in a figure that many acknowledge to be a fiction."

"Oh, but there is," Kringle said. "I'm not just a jolly, whimsical figure in a charming suit. I'm a symbol of the human ability to suppress the selfish, hateful tendencies that rule so much of our lives. If you can't believe, if you can't accept anything on faith, then you are doomed to a lifetime dominated by doubt."

Dorey could not believe what she was hearing. This looney old guy was lecturing *her*! What nerve!

When Kringle spoke again, his voice was softer, kinder. "I like you very much, Mrs. Walker. If I can make you and your daughter believe, there's hope for me. If not, I'm finished." He smiled and took Dorey's arm. "Shall we go?"

Dorey brought him to the TV camera. Then she watched his interview.

He was good. Professional. Friendly. Sincere.

And somehow, he made her feel totally mixed-up inside.

An hour later, Dorey's office phone was ringing off the hook. It seemed that the whole city had seen the interview.

"No, I'm sorry, he can't do private sessions," she said into the receiver. "That wouldn't be fair to the other kids — "

Myrna peeked into her office. "Mr. Bedford's on line three," she whispered.

"Excuse me for a moment," Dorey said into the phone. She pressed line three. "Bryan? I've got the mayor's office on hold. What's up?"

Bryan's voice replied, "If I can arrange a reputable baby-sitter for Susan tonight, do you want to do some shopping and have dinner? Say, at seven?"

"I'm not sure what — " Dorey thought about the mayor waiting on the other line. "Oh, okay. Fine. Seven."

Dorey was dead tired as she walked into her apartment that night at 7:01.

Sure enough, Bryan was already there, with Susan and Kriss Kringle.

Kriss Kringle?

"Hello, Mrs. Walker," Kringle said.

Dorey tried to smile. "Hello, Mr. Kringle."

Susan was grinning from ear to ear. "Nobody at school's going to believe this one, huh?"

"If you *have* to have a baby-sitter," Bryan said with a nervous smile, "who's better qualified?"

Dorey kept her silent smile. She had to. If she let it down for a moment, she might scream.

She didn't say another word until she and Bryan left the building and were heading downtown in a taxi.

"It was Susan's idea," said Bryan. "I just think she wanted to have something good to talk about in school, that's all. Having Santa Claus baby-sit for you is a pretty hot topic. If you're angry, I understand."

Dorey stared out the taxi window. "It's okay," she said. "I'm just a little nervous. Kriss isn't the most normal man in the city."

"You're right." Bryan chuckled. "He doesn't lie, cheat, or steal."

Dorey laughed.

She was feeling more relaxed now. The lights of Times Square, the shop windows, the happy families arm in arm — the sights of the season were lifting Dorey's spirits.

Bryan had picked a cozy restaurant for dinner. Afterward they went skating at the rink in Central Park.

As they glided around the rink, holding hands,

Christmas carols played on speakers around them.

One by one, the skaters began singing along. A policeman, looking over the rink, joined in. Then a group of tourists. A chestnut vendor. A street sweeper.

Before long the entire rink area was a sweet chorus.

Bryan was among them, singing his heart out.

And so was Dorey.

It was that kind of night.

In Dorey's apartment, Susan lay under her sheets. For eleven days she'd been dying to tell Kriss Kringle her deepest wish. To test whether he was real.

But now that Kringle was there, she was clamming up. What if he and her mom were in this together? She'd tell Mr. Kringle her wish, and he'd be sure not to get it for her, just to prove he wasn't real.

"There has to be *something* you want for Christmas," Kringle said. "You know, I'm *very* good at keeping secrets."

Susan looked deeply into his eyes.

Oh, well. What did she have to lose?

She got out of bed and took a locked box from her desk drawer. Opening it, she carefully removed a folded photo she'd ripped from a Cole's catalog.

In the photo was a happy family, sitting on the

porch of a house. A father, a mother, and a girl about Susan's age were smiling at each other as if someone had told a great joke. On the father's lap sat a chubby-cheeked baby boy.

She handed the photo to Kringle. "That's what I want for Christmas," she said softly. "A house. A baby brother. A dad. That's all I ever want. If you're really Santa Claus, you can get it for me. If you can't, you're only a nice man with a white beard, like my mother says."

Kriss Kringle was staring at the photo. Susan couldn't be sure, but she thought she could see his eyes moisten.

"Susan, just because every child doesn't get his or her wish, doesn't mean there isn't a Santa Claus."

"I thought you might say that." Susan looked at the floor. "Well, I don't think I'll ever get those things, so it's no big deal."

"May I keep this picture?" Kringle asked.

"Sure."

Kriss Kringle folded the photo up again and said good night. As he backed out of the room and dimmed the light, Susan felt herself drifting into sleep.

"A family for Christmas," she mumbled to herself. "I don't think so."

Bryan and Dorey strolled home, loaded with gift bags. Beneath the clear, star-flecked sky,

Christmas lights twinkled on the lampposts.

"Was that so bad?" Bryan asked.

"I had a great time," Dorey said dreamily. "I should have listened to you earlier. You're a very patient man, Bryan. Most guys are gone after a few moments of me. I guess I'm very . . . *careful* in my life. I don't need to be disappointed."

Disappointed. The sound of that word hit Bryan hard. He knew what Dorey meant. She didn't want to get married to someone who would leave her.

Like her first husband did.

Bryan knew one thing for sure — *he* would never let Dorey down.

"I got you a Christmas present," Bryan said as they stopped in front of their apartment building. "I want to give it to you."

"What is it?" Dorey asked.

Bryan pulled a small box out of his pocket and handed it to her. "Open it."

Warily Dorey ripped off the wrapping and opened the box.

It was a ring. With a perfect diamond that glinted in the light from the street lamp.

Bryan waited for her reaction. His eyes were bright with hope.

Dorey stared blankly. Then she snapped the box shut.

When she looked at Bryan, her eyes were on fire. "I don't want a *ring*," she said through clenched teeth. "You have a lot of nerve doing this to me. You trick me. You trick my daughter. This is cheap."

Dorey spun around toward the front door, but Bryan grabbed her arm. "I didn't trick you. I mean it. I want to marry you!"

"You think you can shove a ring in my face and expect to change me?" Dorey snapped.

Bryan had to swallow hard. His patience was running out. "Dorey, I've been dating you for two years. You have never given me any idea how you feel about me! I've done everything I could to try to make you happy. I love your daughter like she's my own. I've loved you, getting nothing in return — never *asking* anything in return. I put my faith in you."

"You're a fool!"

"At least I'm not living a life of doubt!" Bryan shot back.

Dorey pulled her arm away and ran toward the building. Her face was red with fury. She took a present out of her shopping bag and hurled it at him.

Then, fighting tears, she stormed through the door.

11.

Bryan slumped on the park bench across the street from his building. He opened the jewelry box and gazed at the beautiful ring he'd bought.

In a few moments, Kriss Kringle walked out of the building. "Mr. Kringle!" Bryan called out.

Smiling, Kringle crossed the street toward him.

"How was your night?" Bryan asked.

"Very pleasant," Kringle said. Raising an expectant eyebrow, he continued, "You didn't call me over here to ask me that. What about our plan — me baby-sitting so you could have a date with Mrs. Walker?"

Bryan sighed. "Your idea was good, Kriss. It just didn't work. We had a good time, but the problem was, I . . . *improved* on your idea a little bit. I bought her an engagement ring."

Kringle grimaced.

53

"She didn't like it," Bryan went on. "Actually, she said she doesn't like what the ring *stands* for."

"Perhaps your timing wasn't particularly good," Kringle suggested.

"Not at all." Bryan snapped the box shut. "You know, Dorey doesn't tell me too much about herself. But I do know she was married in college. Her husband had problems. When Susan was born, he took off and hasn't been heard from since."

Kriss Kringle nodded sympathetically. "And she doesn't want her heart broken again."

"I thought if I gave her a ring, she'd see how serious I was. I thought it would make her feel secure."

"A noble plan."

"She won't open up," Bryan complained. "She's filled with cynical ideas and bitter thoughts, and the real tragedy is she's dragging Susan into it with her."

"Sometimes I think Susan *wants* to believe in me," Kringle said, "but she's a good girl and loyal to her mother's wishes. If I can't convince the mother, I can't hope to convince the child." He sighed. "The Tooth Fairy taught me that."

Bryan smiled at that. "You know, I've been in love with her for two years," he said. "I thought if she'd open up a little, if she'd escape this battle with her past, she'd fall in love with me. But she never will — and I can't spend my life waiting."

"You don't have it in your heart to keep fighting for Mrs. Walker?" Kringle asked.

"I don't," Bryan replied.

He got up and signaled for a cab. As a taxi rolled to a stop in front of them, he gave the ring box to Kringle. "Here. In your line of work, I'm sure you can find some lucky guy to give this to."

Kringle sadly took the box. "I'm very sorry, Bryan."

"I'm a big boy," Bryan replied. "I'll get over it."

"But will Susan?" Kringle said.

Bryan didn't know how to answer that.

Kringle opened the door and stepped into the taxi. "I know what you want for Christmas," he said. "I'll see what I can do."

Bryan nodded and waved good-bye.

As the cab drove away, Bryan felt hope. He believed Kringle.

Thirty-four years old, and Bryan Bedford still believed in Santa Claus.

It was hard to find Tony Falacchi. He had no known address. Jack Duff and Alberta Leonard looked for days.

On December 17 they finally tracked him down.

"Yeah, I did good work for Cole's last year, and they fired me," Tony complained. "They see this old wacko in the crowd and hire him."

"Tell me about him," Duff said.

"The old guy? A loon," Tony replied. "He climbed on my float, he was in my face. I had the cops clear him out."

"Did he get aggressive?" Duff pressed on.

"He had a cane. He tried to give me a whack with it!"

Duff smiled. He pulled a one-hundred-dollar bill out of his pocket. Leaning toward Tony with a big grin, he said, "I've got a little job for you."

12.

"**H**ow's business, pops?"

Kriss Kringle's smile faded. It had been a busy, jolly day at Santa's Workshop.

The last person he expected to see was Tony Falacchi.

But Falacchi was at the head of the line, among all the children, leering. His chin was unshaven, his clothes ragged.

"Sir," Denice said, "this is for children. Could you please step aside?"

Tony turned around to face the waiting line of kids. "That guy up there ain't the real Santa Claus," he announced. "He don't live at the North Pole. He lives in a nursing home on West 114th Street. He's a fake!"

Kriss Kringle was boiling. He started to rise. Denice quickly brought over the next kid in line, a little boy.

"Merry Christmas," Tony said with a cackle. He barged back through the line, elbowing his way past the children.

The little boy climbed into Kringle's lap. He looked up in awe and said, "You live on my street!"

Kringle had cooled down by the end of the day. He left Cole's, tired but happy, and began walking home.

He didn't notice Jack Duff, Alberta Leonard, and Tony Falacchi following hm.

"Hey, goofball!" Tony shouted.

Kringle stopped walking.

Tony swaggered up behind him. "Tell me something, you sorry old cripple. Why's a guy your age playing this kind of game? Are you just a lonely, pathetic old mental case?"

Kriss Kringle turned around. Falacchi was grinning at him.

That did it. Kringle lifted his cane and charged.

Shielding his head with his arms, Tony screamed and fell to the sidewalk.

Alberta Leonard was prepared. Hidden in the crowd, she pressed 9-1-1 on her cellular phone.

"Stop that man!" Jack Duff bellowed.

Reeeeoooo-reeeeoooo!

A siren wailed. Passersby crowded around. Tony moaned on the sidewalk. Alberta kneeled over him.

Across the street, a photographer stepped out

from a shadow and began flashing away.

Kringle stood there, frozen, bewildered at the sudden swirl of events. "I didn't intend to injure him!" he pleaded.

"Get the cane away from him!" Duff yelled.

A man in the crowd took Kringle's cane. Another man and Duff grabbed Kringle by the arms. A police car pulled up to the curb.

"He provoked me!" Kringle said.

"Save it for the cops, sir," Duff replied.

Alberta looked up from Tony with concern. "He's hurt bad." Then, widening her eyes at the sight of Kringle, she shouted, "Wait a second — *you're the Cole's Santa Claus!*"

A murmur went through the crowd. A toddler started to cry. Several parents pulled their children away in disgust.

Kringle looked around him. His jaw was quivering. Duff was yanking on his arm now, pulling open his coat. A policeman slapped handcuffs on him.

Click! Click! Click!

As the policeman pushed Kringle into the car, the photographer's flash exploded in his face.

All he could do was bow his head.

And try to ignore the hurt, betrayed, and angry faces in the crowd.

13.

COLE'S SANTA CHARGED WITH ASSAULT!

The next morning, every newspaper headline in New York screamed the news about Kriss Kringle.

On page two of every newspaper was a full-page ad for Shopper's Express — including the words YES, NEW YORK, THERE IS A SANTA over a photo of Victor Lamberg. Grinning happily next to Lamberg were a smiling Jack Duff and Alberta Leonard.

On the eighth floor of Cole's, a sign hung across the entrance to Santa's Workshop: SANTA HAS GONE TO FEED THE REINDEER.

Denice and Tricia sat by Kriss Kringle's empty throne, sobbing softly with the rest of Santa's helpers.

"Excuse me . . . excuse me, please . . ."

60

Outside, Dorey Walker wound her way through the small crowd at Cole's front door. She gazed into the sad, disappointed eyes of the shoppers.

All she could think about were Kriss Kringle's words. The words that had haunted her all night in her sleep: *"I'm a symbol of the human ability to suppress the selfish, hateful tendencies that rule so much of our lives. If you can't believe, if you can't accept anything on faith, then you are doomed to a lifetime dominated by doubt."*

Dorey knew the words by heart now. She found herself whispering them.

Dominated by doubt? Not anymore.

When she got inside, she sprinted to her office and shouted to Myrna, "Get Mr. Bedford on the phone!"

By the time she took off her coat and threw it on the chair, the phone rang.

"Bryan!" she shouted, grabbing the receiver.

"I know," Bryan's voice replied. "I read the papers."

"I want you to help him," Dorey barged on. "He's at Bellevue, the psychiatric ward. I don't know what's happening, but he's alone and he shouldn't be."

"What's Cole's position?" Bryan asked. "Do their attorneys have an opinion?"

"This isn't about Cole's," Dorey retorted. "This is about someone who's had something very wrong done to him. It's about someone you care about — someone you *believe* in."

Bryan's reply was firm. "I'll get on it right away."

Judge Henry Harper sat heavily behind his desk. He scanned the docket of cases he'd be facing this morning.

His eyes stopped at the first one:

December 19, 9:00 A.M.
New York State v. *Kriss Kringle*

He vaguely remembered Kriss Kringle. He was the old man who spoke to his grandson Ryan at the Cole's Thanksgiving Day Parade. The old geezer who claimed to be Santa Claus.

The court clerk peeked into the empty room and asked, "Do you have a moment for Ed Collins?"

Collins was the prosecutor. He was as crooked as they came. He could be bought with a bribe.

But he liked to share his bribes with judges, too. "Send him in," Judge Harper said.

Collins marched in. His thinning hair was slicked back, his expensive suit freshly pressed. He dumped on Judge Harper's desk a sheaf of papers marked MENTAL COMPETENCY REPORT — JOHN DOE/KRISS KRINGLE.

"Commitment papers," Collins said. "For the Cole's Santa. Sign them. It's a slam dunk. The guy's out of his mind. He failed his mental exam. We'd like it over quick."

"*We?*" Judge Harper asked.

Collins gave a sly smile. "Victor Lamberg."

"Oh, yeah." Judge Harper figured Lamberg was up to something. "Justice will have to prevail, of course," he reminded Collins.

"Of course. The publicity will burn itself out soon. This Kringle has no family. No funds. And I doubt Cole's is interested in supporting a Santa Claus impersonator who's about to be committed to a mental hospital."

"I suppose Cole's difficulties *benefit* Mr. Lamberg, hmm?" Judge Harper asked. "A quick resolution would make his takeover attempt easier, wouldn't it?"

"I'm sure it would," Collins answered.

Judge Harper raised an eyebrow. "Money makes the world go round, Mr. Collins."

"Uh, speaking of money . . ." — Collins leaned closer to Judge Harper — "Mr. Lamberg wanted me to mention that he's aware you're up for re-election in the spring."

Judge Harper smiled. "Tell him I would welcome his support."

The court clerk poked her head into the chamber once more. "A Mr. Bedford here to see you, sir? He says he's Kriss Kringle's attorney."

Collins and Judge Harper gave each other a puzzled look. "Send him in," Judge Harper said.

Bryan strode into the room. "Your Honor, there seems to be undue haste in this case. I wish to protect my client's rights, as I'm sure *you* do."

Judge Harper nodded. "Mr. Bedford, this is Prosecutor Collins."

Bryan quickly shook Collins's hand, then barged on, "If Your Honor please, I request a formal hearing to which I may bring witnesses."

Judge Harper looked at Collins. Collins shrugged. "All right," Harper said. "Thursday morning, nine o'clock."

"Thank you, sir," Bryan said with a grin.

He nodded to Collins and walked briskly out of the chamber.

"I thought you said the old man didn't have an attorney," Judge Harper remarked.

"Does it really matter?" Collins said with a shrug. "It's a hearing, not a jury trial. *You're* the one who has to be convinced."

Judge Harper chuckled. This Bedford guy would have to do a lot of convincing.

After the courthouse, Bryan went straight to Bellevue. He was shown to Kringle's room by a hospital orderly.

"Do you believe Mr. Kringle is dangerous?" Bryan asked.

"No, not this guy," the orderly replied. "Maybe he's a little off the rails, but he's no thug. If he

64

wants to call himself Santa Claus, then God bless him."

The orderly unlocked Kringle's door. "Thanks," Bryan said, ducking into the room.

Click. The door was locked again.

Bryan shook his head. They were locking Kriss Kringle inside. As if he were a menace.

A gasp caught in Bryan's throat when he saw Kringle. Some menace. He sat in a chair, glassy-eyed and slumped, staring out a window.

"Hello, Kriss," Bryan said.

Kringle looked at Bryan blankly. Slowly his eyes focused, and he gave a weak smile. "Hello, Bryan. What brings you out on a miserable day like this?"

"A friend in need," Bryan replied.

Kringle's smile widened.

"You failed your mental exam on purpose, didn't you?" Bryan asked.

"Why would I do that?" Kringle replied.

"I don't know. Maybe you've served people long enough. Maybe you've given all you have to give."

Kringle shook his head. "No."

"Then why did you do it? The charges against you were dropped. The man you hit suffered no injury. You could have been out of here if you'd passed your exam."

"I've disgraced myself," Kringle said.

"I read your transcript. You defended your

honor. You stood up for the dignity of every child. That isn't a disgrace, Kriss. That's decency."

"If I'm seen as a crazy old man, the public will dismiss me and the good name of Santa Claus will be spared."

"That's not true, Kriss," Bryan insisted. "If not for you, there *is* no Santa Claus. You *are* him. Crazy or not, here oɪ gone, *you're Santa Claus.*"

Kriss Kringle shook his head. "Only if the children believe that I am. And what kind of Santa Claus would they be believing in, after seeing and knowing what happened last night?"

"Think about last night," Bryan said. "A man was there to photograph the incident. The man you hit was the man you replaced. One of the men who held you is an employee of Shopper's Express. The *cops* told me this, Kriss. The cops believe in you. A lot of people do. More will when we're finished."

"Finished with what?" Kringle asked.

"We're going to court," Bryan answered. "There's a hearing Thursday to decide if you're to be committed. I'm going to defend you. We've got three days. Together we're going to prove that there is a Santa Claus and you are him!"

Kriss Kringle slapped his knees and stood up. "I'm ready, counselor!"

Dorey barged into Shellhammer's office. She smacked down a piece of paper on his desk. "Has this press release gone out yet?" she asked angrily.

"At noon," Shellhammer replied.

"Cole's is going to deny any responsibility for Kriss?"

"We're not going to endorse what he did. He's obviously unbalanced, Dorey. You said it yourself."

"And if I remember correctly," Dorey shot back, "*you* said it wasn't a problem! This store is going to stand by Kriss Kringle. If they can prosper with him, they can suffer with him."

She spun around and stormed out of the room. Shellhammer bolted up from his desk and followed her.

Dorey wound her way through the hallways, straight toward the office of Mr. Cole.

Shellhammer's eyes popped. There was a board meeting inside. She couldn't —

Dorey pushed through the big oak doors and walked right in.

"We must distance ourselves from this scandal — " Mr. Cole was saying. He interrupted himself and glared at Dorey. "Mrs. Walker, we're in conference!"

But Dorey stepped up to his desk. "I just read your press release and I think you're all a bunch of cowards. You don't deserve to run this store."

The other businesspeople murmured in protest. "You're entirely out of order!" Cole retorted.

"We've spent millions telling people we're the store that cares," Dorey went on. "What do we care about? Profit? Ourselves? What about one of our own, who needs us now? We sang his praises. We said he saved the company and our jobs and careers. Now we want to pretend we never knew him!"

"He's at Bellevue," Cole said. "He's crazy!"

Before Dorey could reply, Shellhammer spoke up. "Who but a madman would spend his life believing that every man, woman, and child on the face of the earth is worthy of his love and understanding?"

Dorey turned around in surprise. Shellhammer gave her a friendly but nervous wink.

Cole's angry expression was softening. "What can I do?" he asked. "The public thinks Kriss is out of his mind. They think he's dangerous."

"We have to change what they think," Dorey said. "If we stand with Kriss, if we challenge the rumors, if we force the truth, we'll win. We'll save Christmas for Cole's and for everybody. Kriss is going into court with the best attorney in the city — and he's going to prove that Kriss isn't crazy."

Dorey took a deep breath. Yes, she said it. And it was true. Bryan was the best.

"I may be thirty years old," she went on, "but today I believe in Santa Claus. How about you, Mr. Cole?"

Cole looked around the room. Everyone else was nodding.

He tapped his pencil and sat deep in thought. Finally, with a sigh, he said, "I'm sixty-three. I believe in him."

Dorey wanted to scream with joy. She glanced at Shellhammer, who was beaming.

Cole clapped his hands. "All right. Cole's stands with Kriss. Sit down and let's get to work."

14.

The new Cole's commercial aired on the morning news. It was simple. Striking. First the Cole's logo, then the words A MESSAGE FROM OUR CHAIRMAN.

Next, Mr. Cole appeared on the screen.

"Today was the first time in seventy-five years that there has been no Santa Claus at Cole's," he said. "Why? Because he is about to go before a court of law where he must prove his identity or face detainment in a mental institution. Questionable circumstances and unknown motives have tarnished his reputation. We at Cole's don't believe the rumors. Cole's believes in Santa Claus. We will stand by him. He has done nothing but serve the children and families of New York City — and the world. We invite you to stand with us and ask yourself one simple question: Do *you* believe in Santa Claus? Thank you and Merry Christmas."

Immediately Cole's telephone switchboard lit up. Operators frantically took calls. One by one, the people of New York spoke up:

"I'm Anne Johnson, from the Upper West Side, and I believe."

"This is Mr. Rodriguez from East 63rd Street, and I believe."

WE BELIEVE.

The message appeared across New York City. On an electronic billboard in Times Square. In the windows of apartment houses. On trucks, tollbooths, restaurant windows, office buildings, movie marquees.

New York City was showing its colors — true blue, for Kriss Kringle.

That Thursday, Kriss Kringle sat in the courtroom next to Bryan, trying to keep his hands from shaking. Curious spectators jammed the gallery seats behind him.

"You'll be fine," Bryan whispered. "All you have to do is tell the truth."

Kringle looked toward the prosecution table, where Collins was busily setting up. "Is there anything I should know about him?"

71

"He doesn't believe in Santa Claus," Bryan replied.

Moments later, Judge Harper emerged from a door behind the bench.

Collins hopped out of his seat. "In the matter of Kriss Kringle, Your Honor, the commitment papers are before you. If Your Honor please, I should like to call the first witness."

Judge Harper nodded.

"Mr. Kringle," Collins said, "will you please take the stand?"

Kriss Kringle smiled as he approached the witness stand. "Good morning, Judge," he said. "How's that grandson of yours?"

Judge Harper swallowed hard.

"Do you swear to tell the truth, the whole truth, and nothing but the truth, so help you God?" the court bailiff asked Kringle.

"I do," Kringle answered.

"Before you begin, Mr. Collins," Judge Harper said, "I want to explain to the witness that this is a *hearing*, not a trial. Mr. Kringle, you do not have to answer any questions against your wishes, or even testify at all."

"We have no objections, Your Honor," Bryan said.

"What is your name?" Collins asked.

"Oh, I'm sorry, I didn't introduce myself." Kringle stood up and extended his hand to Collins. "I'm Mr. Kringle. Kriss Kringle."

Giggles rang out in the gallery.

Whack! Judge Harper pounded his gavel. "Order!" he yelled.

"Where do you live, Mr. Kringle?" Collins asked.

"At the moment I'm at the Bellevue Hospital. It's very comfortable."

More giggles. Judge Harper slammed the gavel again.

"Mr. Kringle," Collins continued, "do you believe that you are Santa Claus?"

"Yes."

Collins looked surprised by the answer. "The state rests, Your Honor," he quickly said, walking back to his seat.

A low mumbling went through the gallery.

"Mr. Bedford, do you wish to cross-examine the witness?" Judge Harper asked.

"No further questions at this time," Bryan replied. He gave Kringle a nod.

"It was very nice seeing you again, Judge Harper," Kringle said as he went back to the defense table.

Judge Harper gave Bryan a sharp look. "In view of your client's statement, do you still intend to put in a defense?"

Bryan stood up. "I do, Your Honor. I should like to call my first witness."

He placed a thick telephone book on the witness chair.

A little girl slowly walked up to the stand and sat on the book. Kriss Kringle smiled. He remembered her well. She was the girl who had asked him for a Patty Pollywog.

"What's your name?" Bryan asked.

"Dorothy Lowry," the girl answered.

"Dorothy, what did you get for Christmas last year?" Bryan continued.

"Um . . . a dollhouse and — "

"Who gave you that dollhouse?"

"Him." Dorothy pointed to Kringle. "Santa Claus."

"How can you be *sure* he's Santa Claus?" Bryan asked.

"Because he looks like Santa Claus. And he's very nice."

Bryan pointed to Collins. "Could that man be Santa Claus?"

"Nope. Santa Claus don't got a bald head."

The gallery burst out laughing.

WHACK! "Order!" Judge Harper shouted.

Collins leaped to his feet. "This testimony is ridiculous. Mr. Bedford is making a mockery of this court. It hasn't been established that there is such a person as Santa Claus!"

"Your Honor," Bryan said, "I would ask Mr. Collins if he can offer any proof that there is *no* Santa Claus."

Collins stared at him. He gulped, then turned to the judge. "Your Honor, I would like to request a recess until tomorrow so that I might adequately prepare to meet Mr. Bedford's challenge."

"Does Mr. Bedford have any objections?" Judge Harper asked.

"No, Your Honor," Bryan replied.

"This court stands in recess," Judge Harper announced, "until nine o'clock tomorrow morning."

Grinning confidently, Bryan sat next to Kringle. "He bought it!" Bryan said. "I knew if I got him angry enough, he'd take the offensive. There's no way, in a court of law, we can prove that Santa Claus exists or that you are him."

"But haven't you given Mr. Collins an opportunity to prove that I *don't* exist?" Kringle asked.

"Exactly. And he'll go too far. Our best defense is to let Collins hang himself. But you have to promise me that you'll speak only when I tell you."

"You have my word," Kringle said.

"Good. I'll see you in the morning."

Bryan walked briskly out of the courtroom. His mind was tumbling. He thought about what he had said, what he should have said, what he would say.

But when he spotted Dorey Walker, standing by the front door, he was at a loss for words. He slowed down and gave her an uncertain smile.

"I wanted to thank you for doing this for Kriss," Dorey said. "I was in the gallery. I don't think you saw me. I don't understand your strategy, but I trust it'll work."

"I still have a long way to go," Bryan said. "But I have a few tricks up my sleeve."

Dorey looked down. "Um, about last week . . . I'm sorry I lost my temper."

"I said some things I shouldn't have," Bryan replied.

"No permanent damage." Dorey looked at her watch. "Well, I have to pick Susan up at school."

"Tell her hello from me," Bryan said.

"I will." Dorey tried another smile. "Thanks again. I suppose I'll see you around if this thing drags on."

"Okay."

Dorey left, waving to Bryan over her shoulder.

Bryan leaned against the door. He felt as if she'd taken a part of his heart with her.

Dorey was dead tired as she tucked Susan into bed that night.

"Is Kriss going to be okay?" Susan asked.

"I hope so," Dorey replied.

"I hope he turns out to really be Santa Claus."

Dorey nodded. "So do I," she said softly.

"Then I'll get what I want for Christmas."

"Well, don't you worry about Kriss. He's going to be fine."

"Because Bryan's his lawyer?" Susan asked.

"That has a lot to do with it."

"Are you still mad at him?"

"I'm not mad at him, Susan."

"You like him again?"

Dorey thought about that a moment. Finally she said, "He's a very nice man. Now get to sleep."

Then she kissed Susan's grinning face good night.

15.

DECEMBER 23, 9:11 A.M.
2 DAYS TO CHRISTMAS

Dr. Arthur Hunter droned on and on about Saint Nicholas. Hunter was a leading religious scholar, and Collins had called him to the witness stand.

Judge Harper listened with his head propped in his hands. There were a few snores in the gallery.

". . . His relics are enshrined in the basilica of Saint Nicola, Bari, Italy," Dr. Hunter said. "His legend is credited with a number of miracles, the best known dealing with saving children from tragedy."

"Miracles?" Collins blurted out. "Do you believe in miracles, Dr. Hunter? Extraordinary events in the physical world that are said to be caused by supernatural forces?"

"I can't say I believe in miracles as you frame the term," Dr. Hunter replied.

Collins paced the floor. "Dr. Hunter, is it not true that in 1969 the Church dropped Saint Nicholas's feast day from the calendar?"

"That's correct."

"In essence, the Church walked away from Saint Nicholas," Collins declared. "So would they not also walk away from the pop-culture figure based on him — Santa Claus?"

"I would presume so," Dr. Hunter said.

"No further questions," Collins announced.

Kriss Kringle seemed ready to burst. Bryan eyed him cautiously. He hoped Kringle would live up to his promise.

The next witness was Air Force Commander Charles Colson.

"Have you ever been to the North Pole?" Collins asked him.

"Yes sir," Commander Colson answered crisply. "In 1972 and again in 1984. I explored the region extensively."

"Did you ever come across any evidence of dwellings, animal pens, barns, workshops — any settlement whatsoever?"

"None, sir."

"In your opinion, would it be possible in that region for an individual such as Mr. Kringle to *create* a settlement large enough to manufacture at least one toy for each of the earth's one-point-seven billion children?"

"No, sir."

Collins looked smugly at Kriss Kringle. "No further questions."

Kringle suddenly rose to his feet. "There isn't any way the gentleman could have seen my workshops," he shouted. "They're invisible!"

"Kriss? Sit down, please," Bryan hissed.

Kringle sat. "Mr. Collins is completely mistaken!" he said to Bryan. "My workshops don't exist in the physical world. They're in the dream world. I thought this was understood."

"Let me be the lawyer," Bryan insisted.

The courtroom doors swung open. In walked a man leading a reindeer.

A huge gasp went up from the gallery.

Judge Harper's jaw dropped. "Mr. Collins, what is the meaning of this?"

"This is a reindeer, Your Honor," Collins said. "I'd like the court to see if Mr. Kringle can make it fly."

"He's baiting you," Bryan whispered to Kringle. "He wants you to lose your temper. He wants you to act crazy. Remember that!"

Kriss Kringle stood up. He smiled calmly. "I'd love to oblige you, Mr. Collins, but I can't make the reindeer fly."

"I didn't think so," Collins said.

Bryan sighed with relief.

"They only fly on Christmas Eve," Kringle declared.

Laughter resounded in the gallery. Bryan cringed.

Collins's eyes lit up. "Of course." He turned triumphantly to the judge. "Your Honor, the state of New York does not want to destroy a colorful myth. But this hearing isn't about mythology. It's about the mental competency of a man who believes himself to be a myth. Every sensible person in this courtroom would have to conclude that Mr. Kringle is, regrettably, insane."

Kringle's face was turning red with anger. Collins glanced at him, then continued: "As a sworn guardian of the law, as a citizen, and as a father, I maintain that this man, who masquerades as a figure of warmth and generosity for profit — "

Kringle bolted up from his seat. *"That's not true!"*

"Kriss! Sit down, please!" Bryan urged.

Judge Harper banged his gavel. "Mr. Kringle will refrain from comment, or he will be removed from the courtroom!" he commanded. "Continue, Mr. Collins."

"It is my wish that Mr. Kringle come under the supervision of the state, so that the children of New York are not put at risk." He turned and looked directly at Kringle. "No one wants to wait until Mr. Kringle injures a child before we act."

Kriss Kringle started to rise. Bryan held him back, but Kringle slapped his hand out of the way.

Collins grinned with anticipation, waiting for Kringle to seal his own doom.

"HEY, YOU BIG JERK!"

The entire courtroom turned toward a high-pitched voice in the back of the gallery.

Susan Walker was standing up in her seat. *"MR. KRINGLE'S THE NICEST MAN IN THE WORLD!"* she yelled out. *"HE'D NEVER HURT ANYBODY!"*

Dorey pulled her daughter down into her seat. The gallery sounded like a hockey game now. People whooped and hollered.

Whack! Whack! Whack! "Order! Order!" Judge Harper shouted.

Kriss was looking over his shoulder at Susan. His eyes were bright with pride and thanks.

Collins walked up to the bench. "The state rests, Your Honor."

As Collins went cockily back to his table, Bryan winked at him and whispered, "Thanks."

Collins looked quizzically at him.

"I had nothing," Bryan said. "My only defense was your offense." He rose to his feet, ignoring Collins's befuddled face. "Your Honor, I have no further witnesses. I rest my case."

Now it was Judge Harper's turn to look befuddled.

Bryan knew it looked unusual — a defense attorney, just *giving up.* But he had to stick with his strategy.

"I shall render my opinion on this matter at noon tomorrow," Judge Harper announced. "Until that time, this court is in recess!"

WHACK!

The hearing was over.

16.

DECEMBER 24, 11:45 A.M.
1 DAY TO CHRISTMAS

DESTROYING SANTA CLAUS:
YOUR TAX DOLLARS AT WORK!

SANTA CASE: TOO MANY NUTS
IN THE JUDICIAL FRUITCAKE?

IS SANTA SUNK?

AT NOON TODAY SANTA CLAUS NEEDS
YOUR HELP!

The headlines lay across Judge Harper's desk. He had had a day to think about it. Now it was almost time for his decision.

Harper looked glumly out his window. He was not alone. Behind him, Prosecutor Collins sat at the edge of a desk. On a sofa were Jack Duff and Alberta Leonard.

Perched on a chair, Victor Lamberg glowered at Harper like a vulture.

"You saw the morning papers?" Lamberg growled.

Judge Harper nodded meekly.

"Mr. Collins has done his work well," Lamberg continued. "A little *too* well."

Collins gulped and looked away.

"My grandchildren think I'm a scrooge," Judge Harper remarked. "The court clerk gave me a dirty look."

"The only way out is to declare this man insane," Lamberg said flatly. "If you'd done it at once, as Mr. Collins told you — "

"*I'm* the judge, Mr. Lamberg," Harper said. "A prosecutor doesn't tell me what to do."

Collins chuckled. "There's no way out, Harper. You can't make a decent legal argument for Santa Claus. You'll look like an even bigger fool than you already do."

"What about the people?" Judge Harper asked. "What'll *they* think of me?"

Lamberg gestured toward a leather briefcase on the desk. "There's a hundred thousand dollars on your desk. Does it really matter?"

Judge Harper took a deep breath. He looked at his watch.

Two minutes until noon.

Lamberg got out of his chair and lifted a newspaper off the desk. "How many people do you think are going to fall for this Cole's publicity stunt? A handful of nuts . . . some kids. Be smart, Harper. Put this guy away and let's get this thing behind us."

Snap! Lamberg unlocked the fasteners on the briefcase. He pulled it open.

The smell of new money rushed into the air. Judge Harper stared at thickly packed piles of crisp hundred-dollar bills.

His eyes darted toward his watch again.

11:59.

One minute.

Judge Harper walked to his window again. Outside, the first snow of the year was gently falling. It muffled the car noises, the roar of the crowd. . . .

Judge Harper's eyes narrowed. What a crowd. People clogged the sidewalks, the streets. They stood by office windows, on top of cars. They emerged from the subways, looking at the courthouse.

And they were *roaring*. All of them. He couldn't tell what they were saying. But he knew what was on their minds.

Judge Harper spun around. Lamberg was glaring at him, his eyes bloodshot and eager.

Beep! went Harper's watch.

It was noon.

Sweating time.

The roar outside was rising in intensity. The snow was falling thick and fast.

Judge Harper walked to his desk. He plunged his hand into the briefcase and picked up a fistful of cash.

One hundred thousand dollars. More than a year's honest work.

He examined one of the bills, flipped it over, stared at the inscription on the back: IN GOD WE TRUST.

Clenching his jaw, Judge Harper marched into the courtroom.

17.

DECEMBER 24, 12:01 P.M.

The gallery was jam-packed. And noisy.
They all fell silent as Judge Harper stood at the bench.

He held the money in the air. "This is a one-hundred-dollar bill," he announced. "It is issued by the Treasury of the United States of America and is backed by the government. Upon inspection you will see the words IN GOD WE TRUST. While we are not here to prove that God exists, we *are* here to prove the existence of a being just as invisible and yet just as present."

He lowered his voice. In the eerie hush, every syllable echoed to the back row. "On faith and faith alone, the federal government has put its trust in God. What guides the government? The will of the people. If the United States of America can issue its currency bearing a declaration of trust in God — without demanding physical evidence of God's existence — then the state of New York can accept, by a similar demonstration of the faith of its people, that Santa Claus does exist, and that he is Kriss Kringle."

Whack! He smashed down the gavel with all his strength. "Case dismissed!"

The gallery exploded with cheers. Bryan jumped to his feet and wrapped Kringle in a bear hug.

The court clerk opened a window and shouted to the throng in the streets: *"CASE DISMISSED! SANTA CLAUS WINS!"*

Like a rumble of thunder, the crowd's cry swept up and down the street.

As Bryan let go of Kriss Kringle, he came face-to-face with Prosecutor Collins.

Collins broke into a smile and extended his hand. "Congratulations, counselor."

"Thank you," Bryan replied, grasping Collins's hand.

"Merry Christmas, Mr. Kringle," Collins said. "My children wanted me to remind you not to forget to stop by our house tonight."

"I will not forget," Kringle assured him.

"We're in Stamford. Thirty-one thirty-three Brompton Road. Big white house."

With a nod, he took off.

"Well, Kriss, you're free," Bryan said. "I don't know how much help I was, but that's not important."

"You came to my defense," Kringle replied. "Without you, I'd have been put away without a peep."

"The truth is, Kriss, it was Dorey's idea. She called and asked me to help you."

"*Dorey* did?"

Bryan nodded. "You made a believer out of her."

Kringle's eyes welled up. "That's such good news!"

"You made a believer out of everybody," Bryan continued.

"Not everybody," Kringle said. "There are still a few who don't believe. One in particular."

"Kriss!"

At the sound of Dorey's voice, Bryan began collecting his papers on the defense table.

Dorey and Susan Walker plunged through the crowd. Dorey threw her arms around Kringle. "I'm so happy for you, Kriss!" she cried.

Susan turned toward Bryan. "Way to go, Bryan."

"Thank you, Susan," Bryan replied.

Dorey pulled away from Kringle and smiled at Bryan. "Congratulations," she said.

"Thank you, Dorey." Bryan offered his hand, and Dorey shook it.

Susan and Kriss Kringle exchanged a hopeful look.

"Well," Bryan said, "have a merry Christmas."

"You, too," Dorey answered.

For a moment, no one said a word. Then Dorey took Susan's hand. "We'll let you go," she said to Kringle. "Merry Christmas and good luck."

With an exchange of Merry Christmases all around, Dorey and Susan headed for the door.

Susan's eyes were full of disappointment. As she glanced at Kriss Kringle one last time, he gave her a confident wink.

Bryan shut his briefcase. "You want to share a cab home, Kriss?"

"Home? Oh, no, not tonight. I'm going to be very busy."

Bryan laughed. "Christmas Eve. That's right."

"My deepest thanks, Bryan. I shall never forget you. In all my travels past and future, I won't find as good a friend as you. Merry Christmas."

"Merry Christmas."

Kriss Kringle turned away. With a bounce in his step, he went out the door.

The crowd had emptied. Bryan stood alone in the courtroom.

He picked up his briefcase and left.

His footsteps echoed hollowly on the tiled floor.

18.

DECEMBER 24, 3:01 P.M.

Victor Lamberg threw the afternoon newspaper onto his desk. He turned it so the headline faced Jack Duff and Alberta Leonard:

SANTA LIVES!

"This is going to blow up in my face, isn't it?" Lamberg asked.

Neither Duff nor Alberta had an answer for him.

"I lost bigger than I ever thought I'd win," Lamberg mumbled.

"There was a lot of pressure," Duff said. "Who knew what the judge would do when he was faced with having to put Santa Claus in the nuthouse?"

"*He isn't Santa Claus!*" Lamberg thundered. "What's the matter with everybody? There *is* no Santa Claus!"

He stalked to the window and stared out.

Alberta looked at Duff. She pulled a button out of her pocket and showed it to Duff.

He squinted and read the words on the button: I BELIEVE IN SANTA CLAUS. Right under the Cole's logo.

Duff stifled a laugh. He looked at Lamberg's back, then quickly opened his suit jacket.

The same button was pinned to his own vest.

A light on Lamberg's phone began to flash. His secretary leaned into the office and said, "Mr. Lamberg? Your granddaughter's calling."

Lamberg turned from the window. His face was creased with worry. He looked suddenly broken, old, and frail.

"Is she angry?" he asked.

When she arrived home from work, Dorey noticed a small blue envelope in the mail. On it, the words To DOREY — URGENT were written in an unfamiliar handwriting.

She ripped open the envelope and read the message inside:

MEET ME AT ST. PATRICK'S
AFTER MIDNIGHT MASS.
                    BRYAN

After wandering around the city, Bryan arrived

at his office late that evening. He noticed a light-blue envelope on his desk, marked To Bryan — URGENT.

On the inside was a note:

> Meet Me at St. Patrick's
> After Midnight Mass.
>   Dorey

That night, before going to bed, Susan gazed out her bedroom window. Snow fell steadily, muffling the street noise below. She looked into the grayish-white sky. She couldn't see much because of the snow.

Not that she expected to see anything. After all, Christmas Eve was a night just like any night.

She plopped her head on her pillow and tried to sleep.

Dorey arrived at the cathedral well past midnight. She was grateful an elderly neighbor had agreed to baby-sit.

What could Bryan have wanted? The service was *over*. The congregation was straggling onto Fifth Avenue, humming Christmas carols and chatting.

Dorey went inside. Her eyes were drawn upward. The walls seemed to rise into the heavens. As she walked up the aisle, her footsteps rang out in the empty cathedral.

She approached the altar. A priest appeared, smiling at her.

This had to be a mistake.

Footsteps clattered behind Dorey. She turned.

Bryan was standing in the front door. He looked just as bewildered as Dorey felt.

Suddenly the organ started playing a wedding march.

Dorey jumped back, startled.

Bryan wandered up the aisle toward her, looking all around — at the organist, the stained-glass windows, the empty pews. . . .

His eyes met Dorey's.

The priest walked forward. He stood in front of the altar as Bryan approached.

"Is someone getting married?" Bryan asked.

"Not that I know of," Dorey replied. "Did you arrange this?"

"No. *You* did."

"I did?"

"You didn't?"

Dorey shook her head. "I didn't. Did you?"

"I didn't." Bryan looked at the priest. "Father?"

The priest held up his Bible. "You're ready?"

"For what?" Dorey asked.

"To get married?" The priest raised an eyebrow in confusion.

Dorey looked at Bryan. Bryan looked at Dorey.

The priest handed Bryan a ring.

A wedding ring.

At that moment, both Dorey and Bryan knew who had set this up.

The one person in the world who knew them the best.

Bryan took Dorey's hand. She did not let go.

They turned to the priest and waited for him to begin.

19.

DECEMBER 25, 7:17 A.M.
CHRISTMAS DAY

She didn't know what she expected to see under the tree.

All she knew was that she didn't get what she wanted.

Susan sat silently in front of her Christmas tree. Presents were piled underneath. That was nice. But they were exactly the same ones that had been there the night before. In the same arrangement.

Which made perfect sense. Kriss Kringle was a nice man, not a miracle worker. He'd have his job back next year, and that was what the whole thing was about, wasn't it?

She glanced at the glass Santa ornament on the tree. She narrowed her eyes. It seemed to be *glowing*.

The light jittered and jumped. It left the ornament and hovered on the wall.

Susan's eyes followed the light as it shot upward to the ceiling, then back down again, then across the wall, around her, behind her . . . and right back to its source.

A polished gold ring. On her mom's finger.

Susan looked up slowly. Her mom was dressed in a robe, sipping coffee, leaning against the living room archway.

Wearing a ring.

"Holy smokes . . ." Susan muttered.

"I have something to tell you," Dorey said gently.

Bryan walked in behind her.

Susan's grin was brighter than the Christmas tree. *He* was wearing a ring, too!

"What did you get for Christmas, Susan?" Bryan asked cheerfully.

Susan didn't answer. She ran toward her mother and threw her arms around her waist.

Her Christmas wish had come true.

There *was* a Santa Claus!

Hours later, Susan was in the back of a cab with her mom and her new stepfather. Outside, fresh snow blanketed snug suburban houses and weighed down tree branches.

"Susan, I know what you asked Mr. Kringle for," Dorey said, "but that's *not* why we're going to the house."

"We're going to the house they showed in the

catalog, right?" Susan asked. "That's the house I told him I wanted!"

Dorey rolled her eyes. "We're going there because it *snowed* and the house is very pretty and Mr. Shellhammer wants to take some photos for next year's Christmas catalog." She folded her arms and grumbled, "Which I think, by the way, is awfully bold of him. It *is* a holiday."

"And a honeymoon," Bryan reminded her.

Susan shook her head. "You're wro-ong, Mom."

The taxi rolled into the driveway of the house. Dorey looked around for the photographer's van, but it wasn't there. The house looked deserted.

"Where is everybody?" she asked, getting out of the cab.

Susan noticed the mailbox at the end of the drive. The name WALKER-BEDFORD was painted on its side.

As Dorey approached the front door of the house, it opened. Shellhammer stood there, smiling. He held out a set of keys toward her. "You got a bonus."

"I knew it!" Susan screamed.

"Wh-what do you mean?" Dorey stammered.

"It's your house," Shellhammer replied. "Cole called me at one o'clock in the morning. He said he wanted to buy you and your husband — " He looked at Bryan. "Did you get married?"

Bryan nodded. "Last night."

Dorey stared numbly at the house. "I can't believe it," she said under her breath.

"Congratulations," Shellhammer said to Bryan. "Was this planned?"

"No," Bryan answered.

"I can't believe it," Dorey muttered again.

"You saved Cole's and we're all grateful," Shellhammer said. "Mr. Cole would be here himself but . . . well, he's the chairman and he has me to do these sorts of things for him." He turned to his car. "Bye-bye."

"Thank you, Donald," Dorey said. "I don't know what to say except Merry Christmas."

As Shellhammer drove off, Bryan pulled a wad of bills from his pocket and paid the taxi driver.

"How did you get a free house?" the driver asked.

"I'm Santa Claus's attorney," Bryan replied.

The cab driver quickly backed away.

Bryan put his arms around Susan and Dorey. The three of them headed into their new home.

They stopped just inside the front door.

A huge Christmas tree stood in the corner, glowing with lights, tinsel, and ornaments. A fire crackled in a brick fireplace. A puffy armchair, a sofa, a thick Oriental rug — the room was decorated with Cole's finest furnishings.

"This is the house I asked Kriss for, and he got it for me," Susan said. "And he got me a dad. The third thing, I'll just have to wait for." She looked at Dorey. "But he'll get it for me, won't he?"

"If Kriss said he'd get you something," Bryan answered, "I'll bet it's already on the way."

"I guess there's no doubt about it — he's real!" Susan was beaming. "I'm going up and look at my new room. Excuse me."

As she sped up the stairs, Dorey called out, "Susan?"

Susan looked over the stairway railing. "What?"

"What else did you ask Mr. Kringle for?"

"A baby brother. See ya."

Dorey turned slowly to Bryan.

Together they both looked down at her tummy.

EPILOGUE

San Francisco was cool and cloudy. In the Brewster Nursing Home, some of the elderly tenants were taking ornaments off the tree.

At the front desk, the clerk said to a new applicant, "It's a comfortable place. We have very few complaints."

Kriss Kringle looked around and nodded. "It'll do just fine."

"Mrs. Brewster will sign you in," the clerk replied. "Down the hall, first door on your right."

As Kriss walked away, the clerk called out, "Excuse me, sir. I didn't catch your name."

"Kringle. Kriss Kringle."

The clerk's smile drooped.

Kriss Kringle winked. Then he turned and walked to his room.

It had been a long night and he was very, very tired.